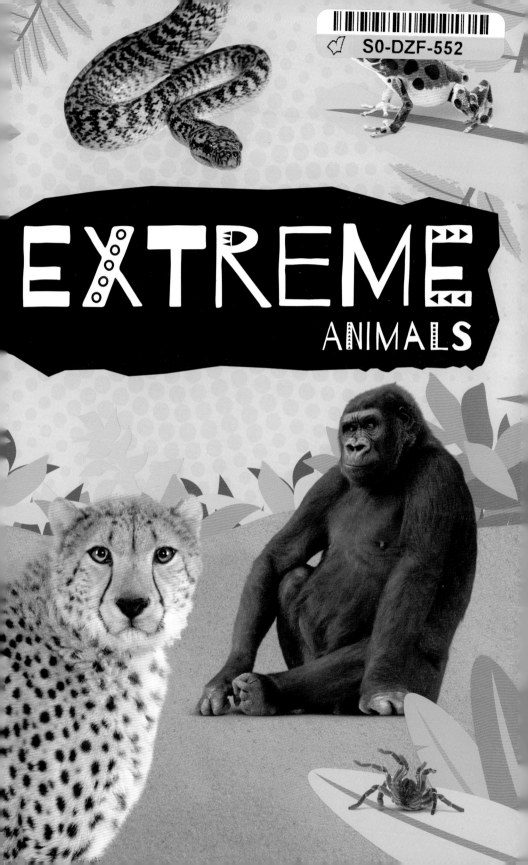

EXTREME
ANIMALS

LETTER TO PARENTS

Dear Parents,

Extreme Animals is an engaging early reader for your child. It combines simple words and sentences with stunning photographs of real animals. Here are some of the many ways you can help your child learn to read fluently.

Before Reading
- Look at the book's cover together. Discuss the title and the blurb on the back.
- Ask your child what he or she expects to find inside.
- Discuss what your child already knows about the animals in the book.

During Reading
Encourage your child to:
- Look at and explore the pictures.
- Sound out the letters in unknown words.
- Use the glossary to learn new words.

Ask questions to help your child engage more deeply with the text. While it's important not to ask too many questions, you can include a few simple ones, such as:
- Can you point to the Komodo dragon's claws?
- Would you like to meet this animal? Why or why not?
- How do you think this insect got its name?

After Reading

- It is important to ensure that your child understands whole sentences and pages as well as individual words. As a comprehension check, ask a few questions about the content and encourage your child to tell you about the book.
- Provide opportunities for your child to read and reread the book. Praise your child's effort and improvement.

Sight Words

This page provides practice with commonly used words that children need to learn to recognize by sight. Not all of them can be sounded out. Familiarity with these words will increase your child's fluency.

Picture Dictionary

This activity focuses on learning vocabulary relating to extreme animals. All the animal names are featured in the book.

Glossary and Index

Encourage your child to use the glossary and index. Explain their purposes and that the entries are in alphabetical order. When your child is reading the book, point out that the words in bold type are the ones that are defined in the glossary.

CHEETAHS

Cheetahs are big cats with spotted fur coats. They are the fastest land animals in the world.

long tail

strong legs

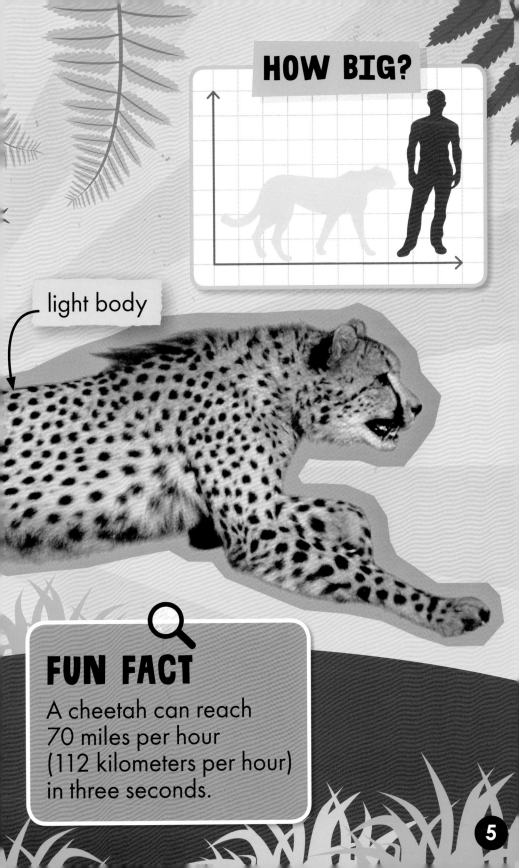

HOW BIG?

light body

FUN FACT

A cheetah can reach
70 miles per hour
(112 kilometers per hour)
in three seconds.

GORILLAS

Gorillas are the largest apes in the world. They live in families of up to 30 members.

FUN FACT

Male gorillas have silver fur on their backs. They are called silverbacks.

silver
fur

HOW BIG?

GREAT WHITE SHARKS

Great white sharks are large, powerful ocean **predators**. They eat fish, seals, turtles, and dolphins.

teeth

HOW BIG?

eye

fin

FUN FACT
These sharks can smell seals two miles (three kilometers) away.

ANACONDAS

Anacondas are the world's heaviest snake. They can weigh up to 220 pounds (100 kilograms). That's nearly as heavy as a warthog.

forked tongue

HOW BIG?

spots

FUN FACT

Anacondas hunt large animals such as deer and wild pigs.

scales

11

PIRANHAS

Piranhas are meat-eating fish with sharp teeth. They live in jungle rivers.

fin

tail

FUN FACT
Piranhas hunt in groups of up to 20.

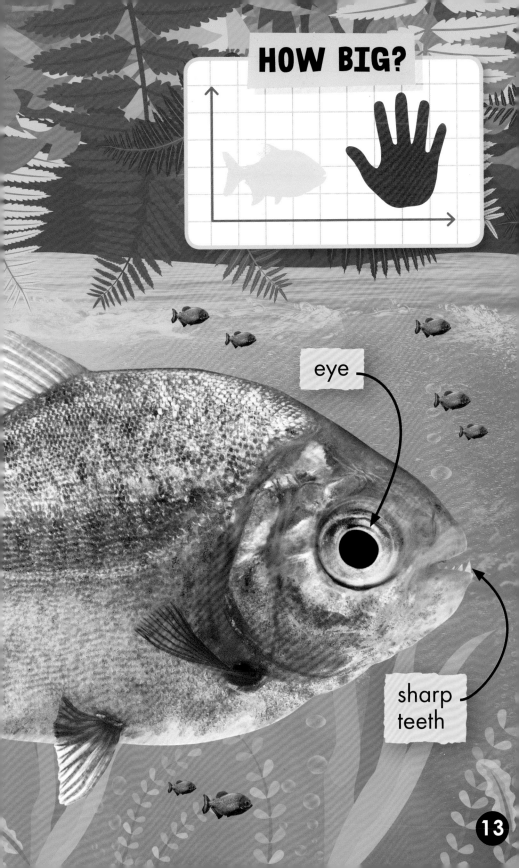

HOW BIG?

eye

sharp teeth

13

TARANTULAS

Tarantulas are large, hairy spiders. Instead of spinning webs, they build **burrows** under the ground.

FUN FACT

Tarantulas can regrow lost legs.

leg

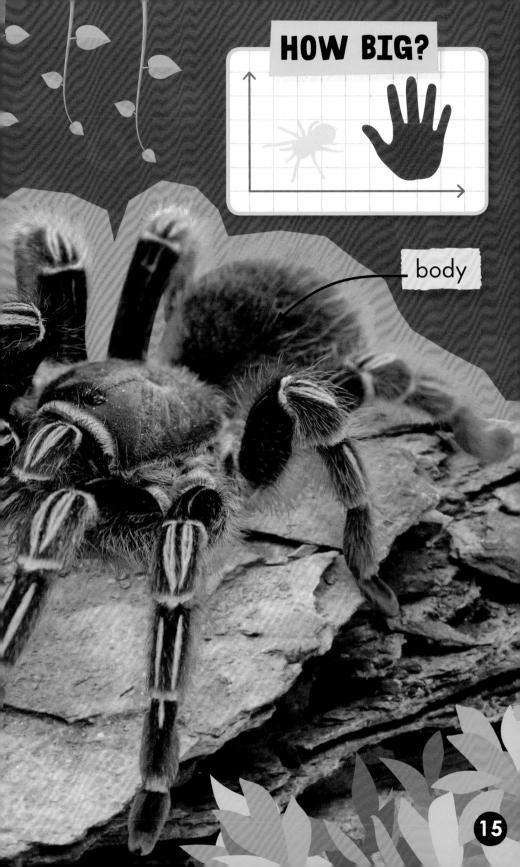

HOW BIG?

body

Komodo dragons are the largest lizards in the world. They can grow up to 10 feet (3 meters) long.

FUN FACT

These lizards use their long, forked tongues to smell and taste.

thick tail

16

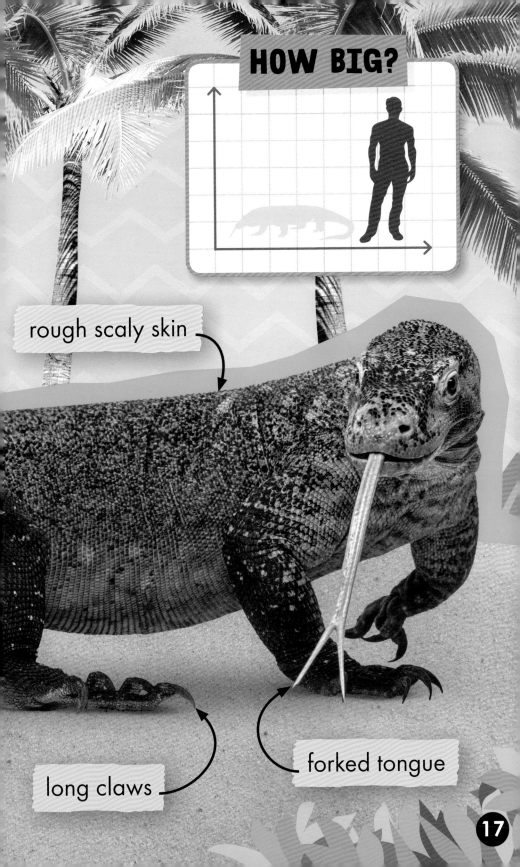

HOW BIG?

rough scaly skin

long claws

forked tongue

BROWN BEARS

Brown bears are fast and strong. They live in many **habitats**, such as mountains, forests, and deserts.

HOW BIG?

FUN FACT

Brown bears are **omnivores**, which means they eat meat and plants.

SALTWATER CROCODILES

Saltwater crocodiles are huge **reptiles**. They eat anything they can find, even monkeys, sharks, and wild boar.

FUN FACT

Adult males can grow up to 23 feet (7 meters) long.

scaly skin

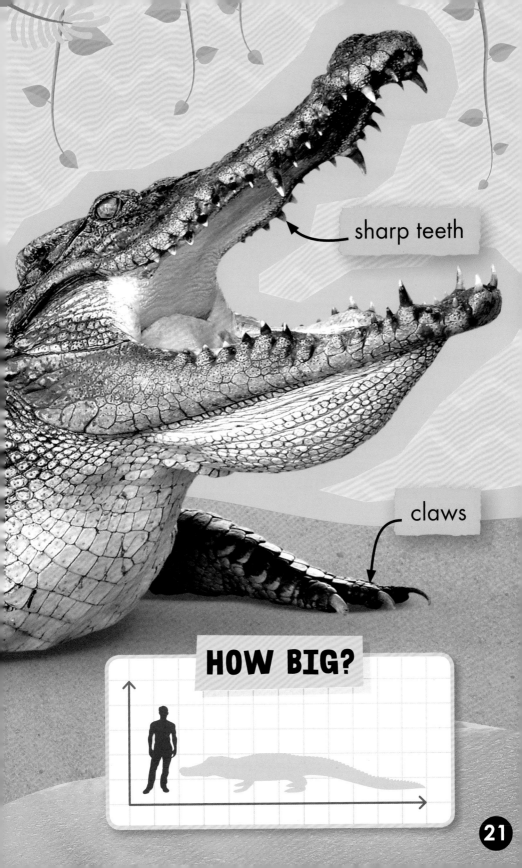

sharp teeth

claws

HOW BIG?

MORAY EELS

Moray eels look like snakes, but they are actually fish. They live in shallow water and around coral reefs.

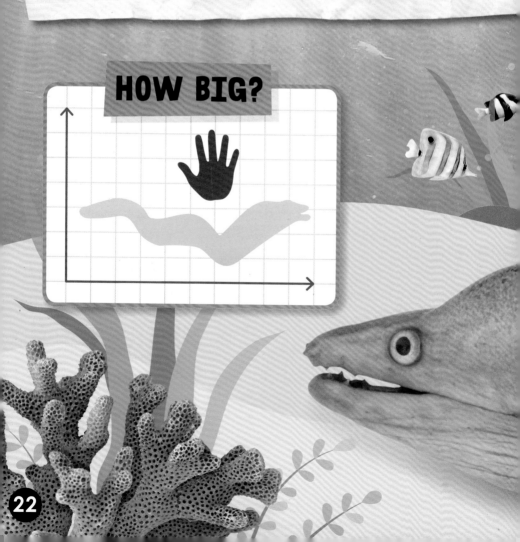

HOW BIG?

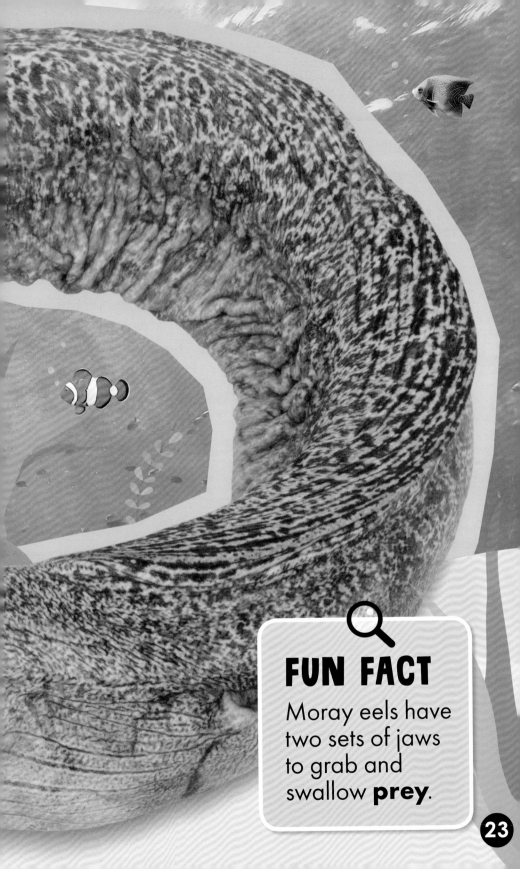

FUN FACT

Moray eels have two sets of jaws to grab and swallow **prey**.

POISON DART FROGS

These frogs live in trees. Their bright colors warn other animals that they are poisonous.

FUN FACT

Rainforest tribes use frog **venom** on the tips of their darts.

HOW BIG?

Nature has many extreme insects.

A praying mantis's two eyes are made up of thousands of tiny eyes.

Blue morpho butterfly wings are so bright they can be seen 3280 feet (1000 meters) away.

Leaf-cutter ants live in colonies of up to 10 million ants.

Goliath beetles can grow up to 4 inches (11 centimeters) long.

was • than • were • same • two • look • but • in • often • find • can • very

SIGHT WORDS

Sight words are words that appear in most text. Practice them by reading these sentences. Then make more sentences using the sight words from the border.

Piranhas **live in** jungle rivers.

Moray eels **look like** snakes.

Brown bears **are** fast **and** strong.

THINK ABOUT IT

How much do you know about extreme animals? Try answering these questions. If you don't know an answer, look back in the book to find out more.

1. What are male gorillas called?

2. Do you think a saltwater crocodile would eat a bird?

3. Would you like to find a poison dart frog? Why?

PICTURE DICTIONARY

Write the correct word under each picture to create your own picture dictionary.

tongue   claws   scales   eyes   tail

anaconda   tarantula   teeth   feet

....

....

....

....

....

....

....

....

....

GLOSSARY

burrow — an underground tunnel that an animal uses as a home

colony — a large group of animals living closely together

habitat — the place where an animal lives

omnivore — an animal that eats other animals and plants

poisonous — an animal that contains poison and can harm other animals

predator — an animal that hunts and eats other animals

prey — an animal this is hunted and eaten by other animals

reptile — cold-blooded animals with scales such as snakes, lizards, and crocodiles

venom — the poison that some animals produce

INDEX

PICTURE CREDITS